MW00717291

Sweet Butter Tea

Ten Phun

SQUAREONE
CLASSICS

Cover Designer and Typesetter: Jeannie Tudor

Square One Publishers
Garden City Park, NY 11040
(516) 535-2010
www.squareonepublishers.com

Library of Congress Cataloging-in-Publication Data
Names: Phun, Ten, 1988- author.
Title: Sweet butter tea / by Ten Phun.
Description: Garden City Park, NY : Square One Classic, an imprint of
Square One Publishers, [2017]
Identifiers: LCCN 2016050749 | ISBN 9780757004476 (softcover)
Classification: LCC PR9499.4.P483 A6 2017 | DDC 823/.92--dc23
LC record available at https://lccn.loc.gov/2016050749

Square One Classics is an imprint of Square One Publishers, Inc.

Copyright © 2018 by Tenzin Phuntsok

All rights reserved. No part of this publication may be reproduced, scanned, uploaded, stored in a retrieval system, or transmitted, in any form or by any means, electronic, mechanical, photocopying, recording, or otherwise, without the prior written permission of the publisher.

Printed in the United States of America

10   9   8   7   6   5   4   3   2   1

Contents

To all the people in this world suffering through injustice.

Acknowledgments

To your Holiness the 14th the great Dalai Lama. Because of you I can write poems and express in words what I feel deep within. This book gave birth a little late to your 80th birthday, but this is my birthday gift of gratitude to you. Thank you, TCV, for nurturing and educating thousands of orphans like me. Part of my heart will always be with you.

Thank you, my beloved Sumola, for your love, simplicity and warmth. I hope this first book reassures you and repays your trust in me.

Thank you, Gathong Akula, for your genuine advice on how to lead a meaningful life, and for showing me the essence of the Dharma.

Thank you, Gale and Victor Yarborough, for your kindness and constant showering of love and financial support on me during my times of difficulties. You believed in me and I wish you both a prosperous life.

Thank you, cho Choenyi Samdup-la, for your delicious homemade food, and for teaching me how to keep myself in one piece.

Thank you, Kerry Wright-la, for giving me the inspiration to hold on to my dreams. Thank you from the depths of my heart for sponsoring me in this publication of my first poetry book. You helped me get my feet more on the ground. Without your support I think I would have been stuck somewhere. Thank you for bringing hope to this fragile being, and for the hours involved in bringing this book from inception to publication.

Thank you, Bhuchung D. Sonam, for your extensive generosity and guidance, and for kindly sharing your years of writing experience with me. I feel humbled to be included among such a respectable circle of writers, and I hope to contribute more in the coming years.

Thank you, Jane-la (Perkins), for your skilled edits and suggestions, and for sharing your keen insights. I wish you the best of luck with your upcoming book on Tibet.

Thank you, Tenzin Rabga Tenzin Zomkyi, John Swinston, Ben Joffe, Thupten Thinley, Tenzin Gyalchoe, Nina Jean, Tegan Teegzy, and Claudia Meca, for reading my poems and making helpful suggestions.

I would also like to thank my literary agency, C&M LifeLine, Inc., and Ted Anders, for their help in turning this work into a reality, and for allowing my words to be shared by so many others.

Thank you, Tenzin Nyima Ringang, for the photograph.

Finally I wish to express deep gratitude to Tenzin Yewong Dongchung, Sonam Dolma Norden, Thupten, Tenzin Kunsel, Nawang Tsephel, and Dorji Tashi-la from Sarah, Tenzin Donsel Gathong for your unfailing support in my life.

Thank you so much to all of you from the bottom of my heart.

Words to
My Readers

My notion of art is a mixture of purity and trash. Art is relative—like painting. You can find pictures in words, words in music, and songs in a canvas. How closely they are all related, wow!

Most of my poems reflect the myriad tunes of loneliness and sadness and the poignancy of our lives in exile. They contain my experiences, observations, and the gentle fragility of this time, and sometimes reflect the bitterly comic. Many were written at night. There are millions of people like me. Every one of us tries to build a home in his or her own heart. It is not that easy.

Many years ago, when I was an inquisitive little monk in one of the biggest monasteries in Tibet, I found my own secret corner inside children's fairytales. I adored this place. It opened my eyes to a bigger world. Reading became a habit.

I read *Snow White* translated into my own language (i.e., Tibetan). I learnt the essence of morality from *The Adventures of Pinocchio*, the wooden boy whose nose grew when he lied; *The Frog Prince;* and *Beauty and the Beast*. When I slept in the abbot's storeroom, I read books and secretly ate milk powder and the small treats my relatives had brought for me. I also listened to music on a tape-recorder. That's how I opened my eyes to the world beyond.

Now here I am, a wandering Tibetan, staying with my chosen brothers and sisters in the shadow of our root guru, safe in the snow-capped ranges of the Himalayan Dhauladhar.

Frankly, I know very little about politics or global affairs. But I understand that each one of us wants to feel good. We dislike disturbances, mental or otherwise. We all like to sleep peacefully after our work is done. I feel that mental calmness is the key to unlocking the door to happiness, and sometimes I achieve it.

I firmly believe any conflict can be solved through negotiation and mutual understanding. I believe in the word "forgiveness" and know it is not a sign of weakness. It is a friendly word that looks to the future. I know it is possible that yesterday's enemies can become today's trustworthy friends.

My inspiration for writing is innate and has been fertilized by observing the efforts of my friends. It has grown stronger over these years of hardship and loss. I never stopped working on my store of words. They enrich my life each day and sink deeply into my soul. I am grateful that words come easily, and am also learning to tame and order them—and myself.

I owe the birth of this book to the sky, the trees, and the mountains, and to the endless sharing with some of the craziest, most humble-hearted beings on earth.

Lastly, I wish that this, my small book of heartfelt poems, might touch you and serve you in some way, perhaps even momentarily soothing that complex place in us all that seems to be seeking a cure.

Ten Phun
Dharamsala, India

Foreword

When Ten Phun was a novice monk at Sera Monastery in Lhasa in the 1990s, a Work Team, comprised of Chinese officials and staff from the local religious Affairs Commission often came to his monastery. The leader of the team would take the young monks to a room and tell them stories, while the senior monks were forced to assemble in a large hall to be treated to ideological lessons under China's "Patriotic Education" campaign. It was there that Ten Phun read the Tibetan translations of *Snow White* and *The Adventures of Pinocchio*. Before leaving the monastery, he stole the two books from its tiny library.

In 1999, his relatives decided to send him to India for a modern education. On the day he left Lhasa, one of his aunts handed him a little red box. "This is what your mother left for you," she said. The plastic box contained a pair of hand-knitted socks and a woolen hat. Years later, in his room at a school for Tibetan children in exile, the box and its contents were eaten by rats.

Ten Phun does not remember his father. His only memory of his mother is of her making a paper boat. "I faintly remember she had a large mole on her forehead," he says hesitantly. The rest is a pixelated image. Both his parents died, his relatives told him, when he was about two.

Today, Ten Phun is a man who walks the crooked streets of exile with scanty memories of his past and abundant challenges and setbacks. The danger of hitting a dead end is a daily possibility. For such a man, writing is healing. It salves the pain and the hurt. This fact is neither a matter of philosophical debate nor a theoretical assumption. However fractured his sentences are, or however he may grasp at words, the truth is that the mere exercise of putting pen to paper creates necessary valves through which the mental void and trauma of dislocation can stream out.

I dont know how old my heart is,
I only know my five-o'-clock shadow tells it all.

I feel the flames on a mother of three.
I smell the burnt skins of monks' flesh.
Flames, ashes.

To tell you how much I miss my hometown,
Should I count my exiled shits and my exiled tears?

From his days in the monastery in Tibet to the poverty-stricken student years in a refuge school to his present phase as a part-time rover, part-time rapper, part-time amateur theater artist and aspiring writer, Ten Phun has collected his share of pebbles along the troubled roads. Where he goes from here depends much on the strength of his character and on our collective view of and response to him—and others like him—who prefer to tread the margins of society without much regard to popular conventions or the righteous advice of distant relatives.

I hope that he finds his gem box, and that the sounds of his words will show him the path across the tortuous mountains to Tibet, where he can eat crunchy noodles with his nieces and nephews. When that happens the circuit will be complete and the missing parts in his hole-ridden memory will be found. He can then, perhaps, write about happier things, such as sailing down the Kyichu River in a yak-skin boat drinking chang and singing songs of love.

Bhuchung D. Sonam
Dharamsala, India

Poems

May you live for aeons and aeons

Your Holiness, I feel like crying
When you sigh in your old monk robe,
When you chuckle like an innocent child.
Your spirit, a humble man.

I feel like crying when I see your portrait
In the barber's shop, and see every rupee
The barber earns is blessed by you.

I feel like crying, when you speak words of hope
And give us the taste of a different reality.
Millions around the world become more open-minded
When they see the peace bird flying high in the sky,
Singing its songs of Love and Compassion.

I feel like crying when our popo-la and momo-la[1]
Narrate stories of two small boys,
The Sun and the Moon,[2]
You are that Sun and the Moon is
Still unaware of his existence.

I feel like crying when people back home
Look up at the moon,
And visualize you in their hearts.

Their feeble voices, their tears and forced smiles
All yearn to receive you back in your home.

I feel like crying when I see you giving a warm hug
To a blind Irishman, praising him
For his tolerance and forgiveness.

I feel like crying when you show immense respect
To the religious brothers and sisters of our time.

I feel like crying when you listen to the views of
Idealists and fill their needy souls
With the courage to have more inner strength.

People in Tibet celebrate your birthday
Behind closed doors and veiled curtains in secrecy,
Fearful of spooky shadows spying like spiders on the wall.

I feel like crying when people from
Mainland China come to India
Just to listen to your words
And to feel your sublime presence.

I feel like crying seeing an empty vestment
On the throne at the Potala, your winter home,
Knowing the pond at Norbulingka is lifeless.

I feel like crying when the burning martyrs
Call out your name before dying.

I feel like crying when I hear you say that
Your religion is kindness.

I can't help crying
When I hear you tell us to never lose hope.

Your Holiness,
I hope and pray that you are with us for aeons and aeons.

---

[1] Popo-la and Momo-la: Tibetan for grandfather and grandmother
[2] The Sun and the Moon refer to the Dalai Lama and the Panchen Lama

No worries, Acha

Fitful dream of last night,
Tearful eyes in the morning
I began rewriting my incomplete poem for you.
I will be back soon, Acha.*
It might take a year or even two,
Five years at the most,
I will be back.
I don't belong here.
I am only a wanderer,
I am a lost soul.
At times I really miss you.
I missed you when I thought life wasn't acting so
Generously with me.
I miss you when I knew that I was
An indifferent boy who
Fought with the neighbour's sons.
I missed you when I knew that I was not reaching my
Promised land.
I remember sleeping with those letters you sent
Me from home.
You said you would come to meet me after several years.
It's been fifteen now,
Fifteen years of my life without seeing you even once.
Do I have to say "No worries"?
I have a heart like an ocean, though,
My soul can easily swim in there.
This ocean is where my feelings linger,
This ocean is where we once swam together.

But the fate of tide is how my life is,
Sometimes rising, sometimes falling,
And that is my definition of happiness.
Sometimes I feel low, sometimes uplifted.
This is the passage of life for me.
But I miss you, Acha,
I miss our days at Norbulingka, where you taught me
How to glide with eagles.
I miss our days near the Kyichu river, where you taught
Me how to float.
I miss our days of going to school together
And when the bell rang,
You were there, waiting outside my class.
I remember you skipping with the neighbour's kids
In the courtyard.
I miss those cartoon books you gifted me on my tenth
Birthday.
I miss that moment when you spoon-fed me
Crunchy noodles.
But I can't cry anymore now, I feel a little
Cold deep within,
Men suffer through warmth and rejoice through cold.
Isn't it so contrary?
But all I could do was pore over those old pictures
Taken ages ago.
Give my imagination a push and write something,
Desperately hoping for our reunion soon.
You must be wondering what I do in this faraway place.
Acha, in a faraway place
I go should-to-shoulder with other men.

I am a product of this showbiz world.
I am a hipster of this little town.
Maybe I am a frog in a well.
But I am not that clean boy with the necktie as
I used to be.
I have had my share of life with assholes, broken teeth and
Scarred faces.
But don't worry,
My friends and I will not end up crippled.
Wild and lost hearts can also rise up and contribute.
Don't be upset with me.
I promise you,
I am going to spur myself with a kick
And when we meet I will entertain you till you cry.
I miss you, Acha.

---

*Acha: Tibetan for sister.

I only know

I don't know if I will ever see my homeland,
I only know someone there misses me.

I don't know how old my heart is,
I only know my five-o'clock-shadow tells it all.

I don't know how to write a constructive poem,
I only know how to pour feelings into words.

I don't know complicated philosophies,
I only know salt is salty and sugar is sweet.

I don't know what the future might hold for me,
I only know I am still breathing.

I don't know how foolish I actually am,
I only know I am very stubborn.

I don't know if fate exists or not,
I only know hurting someone's feelings is wrong.

I don't know whether failure is a part of life,
I only know how to digest it and move on.

I don't know how each second goes,
I only know we will all become old.

I don't know when Tibet will be free,
I only know the birds in the sky fly free.

To China's leaders

I am the son, the grandson
Of the people you thought were barbarians,
The people you treated as monkeys.

Having travelled miles,
Leaving fear, innocence,
Leaving near ones and mothers' milk,
We are far away, with Him.

Five years, ten years, fifteen years,
He will be in his nineties soon.
Will you be there at that time?
You have your fears too, don't you?

You have your longings, your loved ones.
Do you miss your mother?
The flames were burning, the flesh alight.

Did you see with your own eyes
Hidden behind your mask?
Often in my sadness I could not cry,
In my happiness I could not laugh.
I only know forgiveness has its place
Not just from a Buddhist point of view.

So many losses, you might as well know this,
Deep down it never broke us.

The strength you stirred in us
Grew with our patience.
We are still fearless.

We can sing a song of compromise to you
For we are the phoenix.
Someday, we will rise.

Today's light is shrouded by mist. Tomorrow's light
Seems far away.
There will be a sunny day soon.
Our homeland, for us,
Lives only in fragments of imagination and memories.

Friends, when you travel to visit my land,
Please say hello to the mastiffs and Apsos.*
Though, they might bark at you. Even bite.

---

*Apsos: long-coated canine breed, typically white, beige or grey originating from
Lhasa and used as guard dogs in monasteries.

A tribute to Sumo-la

I remember you,
Under the shadow of the sky
And earthly existence.
I remember your palms folded.
I remember your rosary whirling clockwise.
I have seen your secret little corner,
Your little longings in a place, your shrine
Too secret for the beasts to explore.
I remember sneaking into your prayer room,
Interrupting your mantra recitations,
We would recite together.
I remember your Buddha, smiling
I remember your Tara, legs crossed.
I remember you offering the butter lamp
To our guru.
I remember you taking me all the way
From Lhasa to India for a better future.
I remember us jogging near the Potala;
All those memories still fresh in my mind.
I remember us picnicking in Norbulingka.
I was just a kid then,
Careless, innocent, stubborn.
But your love and your warmth,
Your words and your simplicity,
Your grace and your faith were
Undaunted.
I see you now,
Sunken cheeks,

Toothless jaws,
Half blind,
Forehead crinkle-lined.
Time takes its toll,
But your spirit remains.
I can't be there at your side now,
But Sumo-la,* I can sing your favourite song.
Your words are still my benchmark.
While appreciating it all
I can only linger
And try to be a good man.

---

*Sumo-la: Tibetan for aunt.

The secret

There's only one secret,
Buried deep inside each heart,
Among the men of letters,
And in the clouds of criticism.
All men have it,
And each man knows it—
The Truth.

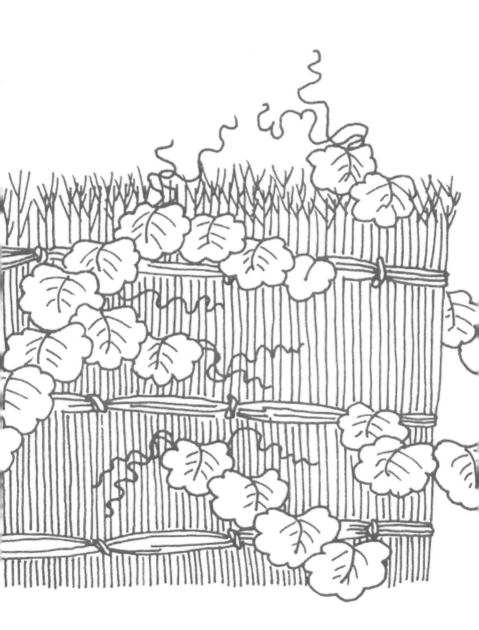

Life is elsewhere

Along the narrow Barkhor street
My kite flies high and free.
It dives above the Potala Palace.
It glides along the Kyichu river.
Dadon's * melody of Lhasa, flowing.
The fresh air, bone-chilling cold water.

I can smell the damp pool,
I can relish the taste of the apricots and apples
Of Norbulingka.
The sky painted so blue,
Prayer flags waving.
My hometown, my life, then.
Everything seemed so refreshing.
Under the dimly-lit candles,

Our bedtime ghost stories, our excitement.
My endearing moments
Now live elsewhere?

Here, in this small town,
I hear about the killing of innocents in some parts,
The news of a natural disaster somewhere else.

I feel the flames on a mother-of-three.
I smell the burnt skins of monks' flesh.
Flames, ashes.
I can see the corpses thrown into a pit.
Unidentified.
Will flowers grow from these brave lost souls?

---

*Dadon: She was a popular Tibetan singer in early 1990s and later had to escape from her hometown Lhasa because the Chinese authorities considered some of her songs a threat to the state. She played the lead in the movie 'Lung-ta' which was based on her life.

Buddha

He pondered on emptiness,
And fed himself tons of truths,
And relaxed, gazing at the wheel of samsara,
Turning, rotating, glittering—
Where the Six Dwellers* are giddy,
Vomiting on the axis,
Collecting filth and falsity,
Stepping on the Four Noble Truths

In a heap of garbage.

Buddha wept.

---

*Six dwellers: gods, demi-gods, humans, animals, hungry ghosts and beings in hell.

Self talk

I talked about attachment,
I thought about love.
These words are really mixed for me.

Mixed with emotions.
Emotions blended with the self.
The self is the spirit
Extending from birth.
Who will question for eternity
But oneself?

All spirits long for love,
Where is that love of ingenuity and purity?
Is love a gift to humanity,
Or a disaster for fools?
Is it the milk of a mother or the kiss of a father?
Is it the wisdom of your enemies or the advice of your
Friends?

Life moves in circles,
Our consciousness, just a blind guest,
Dependency is nirvana.

So where is that absolute answer?

Threesome

He was born in U-Tsang
Grew up with Khampas
And has Amdo friends
If you don't like his accent
Taste his blood;
It's made of tsampa* and chura*.

---

*Tsampa: roasted barley flour, which is the Tibetan staple food.
*Chura: Tibetan for dried cheese.

Destination

Time is a magician,
But the tunnel is long.
My heart is swollen,
My joy punctured.
Life is evergreen,
Yet love is seasonal.
Destinations are many,
Yet the roads are few.
The edges of the hills are sharp.
Truth or dare.
Swim or sink.
Life is not a video game.
My feet are bruised.
My spirit has travelled far and wide
Now the sky is my blanket.

Let it go

When tempests rattle your heart,
Oceans flood your eyes,
Anger rules your mind—
Just let it go.

Let it go like the dry leaves
That dance in the tornado,
Let it go like the ripple on water,
Vanishing.

When thunder distorts your voice,
Volcanos erupt your ego,
Anxiety increases your blood pressure,
Let it go like the rainbow,
That appears after rain,
And slowly fades away.

Let it go like the mother,
Whose child never once showed gratitude.

Let it go like the blowing wind.

Let it go like a fart,
Just let it go.

Simplicity

A farmer's hearty meal,
A poet's circle of words,
The few coins of a beggar,
The silence of a gravestone,
A lullaby's melody,
A kid's paper boat.

Just stay for a while

If you can't be there in person,
Just stay for a while in my heart.

If you can't give me your heart,
Make sure our stories remain sincere.

If the things I did seem off-beat,
Let me remain silent for a while.

If I seem tiresome,
Let me show you my frog jump.

If expectations ruin our relationship,
Let me return to my monkhood heart.

If you think I am so cruel,
Let me sacrifice everything for you.

If love is so impossible in our eyes,
Let's take a walk in the fields.

Stay for a while under this canopy.
Just stay for a while.

Butterfly

There is a butterfly in my stomach.
It flutters its wings and
Makes me laugh.
This butterfly never wants to come out.

Little one,
You stay there inside me,
Make my heart tender.
You creep among my ribs
When my mouth fumes and rages,
Yet you never betray me.

When lonesome feelings reign like a king,
You quietly turn cold.
This butterfly in my stomach needs warmth.
Needs and Wants are not good words,
But a few of these are necessary.

This butterfly often tickles my stomach.
He asks many things from me.
He wants to listen to Canon in D;
When I let him hear my version
He laughs,
Little one, I never wish to vomit you out,
You keep me reckless.

Let it flow

Release a big sigh when you feel it.
Don't imitate, be who you are.
Let your eyelids swell.
Release all your burdens,
Just throw them away.

Go into the pasture of peace
Which is calm and full of colour.
Throw yourself into the river
Against the current, kick the waves,
Take in a stomach full of water,
Spray it out and relax.

Somebody is always there,
Somebody is there to hold you
When you are falling:
Somebody is there for you.

That I believe.

Evanescence

All you could feel are suppressed childish fears,
Now you are wearing them in adulthood's skin.
In deep contemplation, you vow never to look back.
The present, this moment, the sands of the Sahara.

You cross the oasis and leave a few drops for...
Optimism.
Little drops can quench all our thirsts and desires.
You gazed up at the blue stars, saw the comets
And meteors,
Now you wish to fade away from the cherished
Memories
Like an invisible man wandering everywhere.

You hope you leave no remnants or scars in them.
Sacrifice, for you, is a word of commitment.
It is the courage to stand firm when the ground is shaky.
It is being truthful to your conviction.

My art is simple

My art is simple, just to laugh your heart out;
My art is to cook food from the heart;
To speak words from the heart;
To tickle your senses from the heart.
My art gives company with broken stories,
And warmth to cold feelings.
My art is to make you feel the protective umbrella
In torrents of rain.
My art is neutrality;
My art is a mixture of trash and purity,
Impulsive and childish.
My art is about divine madness.
My art is for Anne Frank, the sweetest author
I have ever known.

Silence

Sail of emotions on a calm lake,
Growing stronger within.
Silence is a space where you can
Mend your broken heart.
Inhaling its purity.

Silence is a call to awaken a wiser part of us.
In the core of humanity and understanding
It is where Mother Nature resides.

Silence is like a toothbrush maintaining
Gleaming strong teeth.
Tune of your heartbeat.

It dances in the rhythms of your laughter,
It is a simple gift you can share with your friends,
In silence.
The joy of light-hearted beings.

What more can I write?

I lost the last poem I wrote for you,
Now I just want to sit and look at the rainbow
In the sky.

What more can I write?
I have poured out everything I have within me,
Now I just want to feel the emptiness.

What more can I write?
I don't need to get angry to stand my ground,
This is not a sign of weakness.

Sometimes I go wherever my mind takes me,
My fears grow faint and my love grows steadily.
Now I just need a nap.
What more can I write?

What more can I write?
I feel happy when I feel the ocean's stillness.
I want to take a deep breath.

What more can I write?
Everything is a melody in my eyes,
I want to be naked and eat grass.

What more can I write?

I feel full of writing

I feel full of writing because I need to add more to the
Void of this unpredictable life.

I feel full of writing because it's the first day of Losar
And I am drunk.

I feel full of writing because I have imagination beyond
This bar. All I can do is wander around and share good
Feelings with the fellow seated next to me.

I feel full of writing because I don't want to end my life
Like the stories in fairy tales. It seems too unreal.

I feel full of writing when I listen to Beethoven's
Moonlight Sonata.

I feel full of writing because Rangzen Shonu[1] is now
No more, but they had an impact on me, to keep my
Own narratives.

I feel full of writing because Mao said he did not
Brush his teeth. Tigers don't brush either.
He killed 63 million Chinese people, excluding
Tibetans. Can you imagine that?

I feel full of writing because Bruce Lee said it's better
To practice one kick over a thousand times, to get it right.

I feel full of writing because Buddha never said he took
Responsibility for us. He said we are our own masters.

I feel full of writing because I have seen my friends who
Followed excellence achieve it.

I feel full of writing because I miss friends who got
Addicted and died.

I feel full of writing because I want to go back to the
Times with my cousins and tell them, "Your home is
Where your heart is" I wear my heart on my sleeves
Sometimes.

I feel full of writing because there is the vibe of the
Beat Generation. I salute you Kerouac.

I feel full of writing because Mother Teresa's lifelong
Service to humanity means more than the knock-out
Punches of Mike Tyson.

I feel full of writing because words should be contained
In blood and effort.

I feel full of writing because it's punishable to find
One's soul mate in school. I am against this regulation.

I feel full of writing because I am getting mad in my
Poems, with their melodies, my soul glides everywhere.

I feel full of writing because I feel sorry for the guys in
The 27-club, who died too young to say goodbye.

I feel full of writing because I used to wet my bed like
George Orwell in his boyhood. I had my share
Of lonely times.

I feel full of writing because I am a street guy. I learn
Better when wandering.

I feel full of writing when I remain in solitude to be
Quiet, to control these flying thoughts. I think when
I am alone.

I feel full of writing because writing is for the soul, it
Should not be forced. Like freedom, it should be as free
As the wind.

I feel full of writing because I have my share of
Madness but still find beauty in simplicity.

I feel full of writing because Gedun Chophel[2] drew lots
Of erotic pictures. He was an artist.

I feel full of writing because I dreamt of playing football
For Tibet but ended up playing in the street. I still have
The stamina and inspiration.

I feel full of writing because The Beatles melted this
Fragile heart of mine many times.

I feel full of writing because I was a confused boy in
School. I sang a sad song during the Talent Night and
The audience laughed their heads off.

I feel full of writing because Wang Lixiong[3] dreamt that
He was a Tibetan. He is for Tibet and China. This
Moves me.

I feel full of writing because I've never said I am going
To surrender; I am going to learn from my mistakes.

I feel full of writing because in 1998 I watched
Titanic with my cousin-sister in Lhasa, our last time
Together.

I feel full of writing because for me the purpose of
Living this life is to find my true passion and realise my
Dreams.

I feel full of writing because I believe it is better to train
One's thoughts in a balanced state of mind.

I feel full of writing because Chogyam Trungpa[4] spoke the
Queen's English. I wish I could speak Her English, too.

I feel full of writing because love is beyond my
Understanding, but it fascinates me so absorbingly
That I found sweet bitterness in its pursuits.

I feel full of writing because attachment is like a
Cigarette; lust is like a golden puff.

I feel full of writing because in the silence of the night
I can see my hometown on the wall.

I feel full of writing because Tibet's map is the shape of Deformed cowboy boots, but it is 2.5 million square Kilometers, the source of Asia's rivers.

I feel full of writing because Gedhun Choekyi Nyima[5] was Abducted on 19 May, 1995, when barely six years old. Where is he?

I feel full of writing because pawos[6] and pamos died for Freedom, and I don't know if their spirits Rest in Peace.

I feel full of writing because often in my nightmares, I can Hear the howls of wolves and the thundering of dragons.

I feel full of writing because stories change, and I truly Believe Tibet's story will also change.

---

[1] Rangzen Shonu was an early 1970s exile Tibetan band.

[2] Gedhun Chophel (1903–1951) was a Tibetan artist, writer, and scholar. He was born in 1903 in Rebkong, Amdo, northeastern Tibet. He was a controversial figure and is considered by many as one of the foremost Tibetan intellectuals of the twentieth century.

[3] Wang Lixiong is a Chinese writer and scholar, best known for his political prophecy fiction, *Yellow Peril*, and for his writings on Tibet and provocative analysis of China's western region of Xinjiang. Husband of famous Tibetan poet Woeser.

[4] Chogyam Trungpa (1939-1987) was a Buddhist meditation master and holder of both the Kagyu and Nyingma lineages, the eleventh Trungpa tulku, the supreme abbot of Surmang monasteries, scholar, teacher, poet, artist and originator of a radical re-presentation of Shambala vision.

[5] Gedhun Choekyi Nyima (born 25 April 1989) is the 11th Penchen Lama recognised by the Dalai Lama. After his selection, Chinese authorities detained him and he has not been seen in public since 17 May 1995.

[6] pawos and pamos: male and female martyrs

I met a wise man
in my dream last night

In my dreams last night
I took a lonely breath.
I don't know how I fell asleep.
I was not in the mood for open eyes,
Awareness of howls loosely gripped my eyelids.

Then, in my dream, I met a wise man
Draped in white cloth.
He said that this life of ours is meant for happiness,
He said happiness needs nothing else but you and me.
He said happiness is not just a word in a dictionary.

Maybe the warm person in that dream meant
Contentment.
I answered him with words of curiosity.
Here on earth all religions preach about attachment
And compassion.
He said, "Recently hundreds of innocent kids
Were killed in one region of this earth of ours.
Man killing man, is this the showering of love?
Is this compassion?
Is killing a ritual in your religion?"

I did not answer.
I only know hurting someone is wrong.
He paused for a while then spoke softly.

"My fearlessness lies not in the sharpness of blades,
It is there in your heart and you have to discover it by
yourself."
He told me that if we really want to see the lighter side
Of our awareness,
We have to feel now, act now, compassionately and
Genuinely.

The man I met in my dream gave me his final words.
He said "May peace prevail on earth " three times, and
Then disappeared from the hazy memory of my dream.

Reminiscence

In my dreams I relive my boyhood days,
Running a kite along the narrow streets of Lhasa.
Sailing the paper boat on a river nearby our house.
Peeking into a small CD shop at the corner of
Tomsig Khang[1] and imagining
Owning one while reaching adulthood.

For two yuan of noodles I would stay the whole day
Watching Tibetan movies in a restaurant
Inside Bharkor.[2]
Those memories are enshrined within me.
The pulse of it makes me ponder
the Neverland of my childhood.

The dire times of lonesome living with Wangdue,
Our mastiff,
My little sheep and all my toys.
Under the cool light of the moon,
I would wait to see Tara[3] with her rabbit
High up in the dark sky
I would wish for a divine sage, drifting on clouds.

Am I now a blighted flower or a promising seed?

---

[1] Tomsig Khang: Lhasa's popular market.
[2] Bharkor: Bharkor Street is a very ancient street surrounding the Jokhang Temple in Lhasa. Tibetans perform koras or circumambulations around the temple daily.
[3] Tara: Also known as Jetsun Dölma, a female Bodhisattva in Mahayana Buddhism who appears as a female Buddha in Vajrayana Buddhism.

Exile kungfu

To tell you how much I miss my hometown,
Should I count my exiled shits and my exiled tears?
Should I count my exiled memories and my exiled shoes?

To explain my experiences here,
Should I sing a song of 'Thank you India,'
Or share my message of forgiveness to China?
Should I bear the complaints of my landlady,
And sigh at the grimaces of this cobweb-ceilinged
Room?
Or should I lace my hiking boots and trek home?

There is a monster in your brain

Get rid of him,
Get rid of him now.
There is a monster in your brain,
He wants to share several puffs with you.
He wants to drink your blood.

He is consuming and he is a monster.
This monster wants to see you stay numb, eyes droopy.
He wants to see you struck down on the highway.
Get rid of him now.

He is the small joy of ephemeral longings.
He is the sucker.
Be bold and kick him out
Only then will you be called wise.

There is a monster in your brain.
He is the zipper,
He is the one who tore out your heart,
He is the one who plays with your patience.

He is the one who drives your desires
He is the one who pulls the strings of your
Half-baked life that are infinite in number.

Now come on,
This monster is destructive.
You know it.

Remember how I used to warn you about
The little joys of endless greed?
Sweep him away along with the evil spirits
Of the Guthuk[1] ritual of Losar,
And never look back at him.

The monster inside disfigures you with dark lines
Circling the pouches of your eyes.
Just kick him out like a football,
Wipe him from your mind.
Just let him go and do your own thing.

---

[1] Guthuk is a noodle soup in Tibetan cuisine. It is eaten before Losar, the Tibetan New Year and is focused on driving out all negativity, including evil spirits and misfortunes of the past year, and starting the new year in a peaceful and auspicious way.

Forgiveness

In defense of forgiveness
Forgive the rain that pours down too hard
And ruins lovers' day out in town—
For it brings life to the fields across the way.

Forgive the flowers that fade in time
And ruin the old woman's passion for life—
For they come again when summer again comes.

Forgive the monkey who steals your banana
And leaves you feeling robbed—
For he'll share it with his family and heirs.

Forgive the compassion that forgets its promise
And betrays the saints who believed in it—
For Buddha is too busy to instill his principles.

Garrulous sparrow

Well, you garrulous sparrow,
When will you leave my window sill?

You shit there, and eat there,
You go on dates, and make love there,
You chatter, and debate.

Pray, what nonsense is this?
What brings you here with your loud cacophony?

I pay the rent.
You're an uninvited guest.

Bad girls

Bad girls dream of fantastic worlds
While surviving crushed romances.

Their shiny lipsticks and fat brush mascaras are
As indispensible as pens and books for writers.

They might venture into random thoughts,
But have you ever noticed the aesthetic cocoon
Which wraps their subtle gentleness?
With their brimful energies and quirky senses of
Humour, the spirit of gangsters and lives of Bohemians,
They can be as tactful as they are careless;
For they express feelings in such a way, that they
Draw you into their core.

Inside them, you can feel the artistic expression
Of genial mannerisms;
I assure you, they have hearts
Which have been downsized,
And have been through the storms
Of tumultuous years.
They are not to be blamed for the punches
Life bestows on them.

They stand tall and vigorous on their high-heeled boots
Though kick-ass clouds have weathered away their
Beautiful thoughts.

Their emotions are fragile,
Their hearts, pure with an innocent look;
Sweet memories and tender dreams,
They are the artists,
Living low and high,
The hipsters, the free souls and the fashionistas—
Madness and all.
What is more appealing than their beauty?

Child heart and butter tea

No more wandering,
Read me some poems,
Draw some melody from them.
If you touch my heart,
I will serve you butter tea.

Child heart,
No more bad feelings,
The good, the bad and the ugly
Written on the map of their palms.
You must be tired of walking on the
Road of patience.

Here,
I have prepared butter tea for you.
Have it with me.

Child heart,
Share me a feeling through song,
And I will tell you how much you miss your homeland
While we sip.

Child heart,
In your playful years,
Your Sumo-la poured butter tea with love,
Now you feel it,
And you live it,

The warmth and purity of her being.
My child heart,
This tea is getting cold.
Drink it
With me.

Seasons of life

Autumn days are my joys and freedom,
For the trees, clouds and birds live within me,
The dried leaves of my winter days,
Have long dissolved into fertile soil.
I am a spring flower now,
Ready to offer my life to my guru.
And the summer, my summer, is the
Shining light in my heart.

About the Author

Poet/rapper/actor Ten Phun was born in Lhasa, the capital city of Tibet. After losing both his parents, his aunt enrolled him in Lhasa's Sera Monastery, where as a novice monk he secretly read children's storybooks translated into Tibetan, including *Snow White* and *The Adventures of Pinocchio*. In 1999, he fled to India, where he studied in a Tibetan refugee school. He studied briefly at Delhi University before dropping out to live an artistic life in the hills of Dharamsala. Ten Phun sings, writes, and acts in plays as a member of the only Tibetan theater group in exile.

OTHER SQUAREONE CLASSICS

THE BUDDHA'S GOLDEN PATH
The Classic Introduction to Zen Buddhism
Dwight Goddard

In 1929, when author Dwight Goddard wrote *The Buddha's Golden Path,* he was breaking ground. No American before him had lived the lifestyle of a Zen Buddhist monk, and then set out to share the secrets he had learned with his country - men. This title was the first American book published to popularize Zen Buddhism. Released in the midst of the Great Depression, in its own way, it offered answers to the questions that millions of disillusioned people were beginning to ask—questions about what was really important in their lives. Questions we still ask ourselves today.

As a book of instruction, *The Buddha's Golden Path* has held up remarkably well. As a true classic, it has touched countless lives, and has opened the door for future generations in this country to study and embrace the principles of Zen.

$14.95 • 208 pages • 5.5 x 8.5-inch quality paperback • ISBN 978-0-7570-0023-2

I CHING FOR A NEW AGE
The Book of Answers for Changing Times
Edited by Robert G. Benson

For over three thousand years, the Chinese have placed great value on the *I Ching*—also called the "Classic of Changes" and the "Book of Changes"—turning to it for guidance and insight. The *I Ching* is based on the deep understanding that our lives go through definable patterns, which can be determined by "consulting the Oracle"—the book of *I Ching.* Throughout the centuries, *I Ching* devotees have used the book as a means of understanding past, present, and future events, as well as exercis - ing control over some events. The book highlights hundreds of different possibil - ities we might face in daily life, both on a professional and on a personal level.

For over ten years, researcher Robert Benson worked towards making the English text of the *I Ching* easier to understand and use. The result is a book that focuses on the text's essential meaning and is highly accessible to the modern Western reader. In addition, Benson provides an illuminating history of the *I Ching,* explaining how the text was created, discussing how it works, and exploring its many mysteries.

$17.95 • 352 pages • 6 x 9-inch quality paperback • ISBN 978-0-7570-0019-5

For more information about our books, visit our website at www.squareonepublishers.com.